Earth Always Endures

Earth Always Endures

Native American Poems

Selected by Neil Philip

Illustrated with photographs
by Edward S. Curtis

VIKING

For All My Relations

VIKING
Published by the Penguin Group

Penguin Books USA Inc., 375 Hudson Street, New York, New York 10014, U.S.A.
Penguin Books Ltd, 27 Wrights Lane, London W8 5TZ, England
Penguin Books Australia Ltd, Ringwood, Victoria, Australia
Penguin Books Canada Ltd, 10 Alcorn Avenue, Toronto, Ontario, Canada M4V 3B2
Penguin Books (N.Z.) Ltd, 182–190 Wairau Road, Auckland 10, New Zealand
Penguin Books Ltd, Registered Offices: Harmondsworth, Middlesex, England

First published in the United States of America by Viking, a division of Penguin
    Books USA Inc., 1996

10   9   8   7   6   5   4   3   2   1

AN ALBION BOOK

Designed by Emma Bradford

Selection and preface copyright © Neil Philip, 1996
Volume copyright © The Albion Press Ltd, 1996
Page 92 constitutes an extension of this copyright page.

Special thanks to Joseph Bruchac for his advice.

All rights reserved.

Library of Congress Catalog Card Number: 95-62372

ISBN 0-670-86873-6

Printed and bound in Hong Kong by South China Printing Co.

Set in Bauer Bodoni.

ENDPAPERS: **Pima Baskets** *Pima*
HALF TITLE: **An Idle Hour** *Piegan*
FACING TITLE PAGE: **White Duck** *Hidatsa*
CONTENTS PAGE: **Contents of Arikara Medicine Bundle** *Arikara*

Contents

Preface

Earth always endures.

Just three short words–yet they contain a whole world.

Ruth M. Underhill, who collected hundreds of songs from the Papago in southern Arizona, noted that many of them "seem no more than rearrangements of the beloved words 'rain,' 'wind,' and 'mountain.'" Others are "as clear in contour as a Chinese poem."

The Native American song traditions may remind us of Chinese or Japanese poetry, because the songs are so highly concentrated. The words are honed down to the barest minimum, yet eloquent: sharp, intense, and freighted with feeling. They are so finely worked that they speak across culture and across language, soul to soul–especially in the literal word-for-word translations of a sensitive collector such as Frances Densmore, who recorded "Earth Always Endures" from Wounded Face, of the Mandan.

I say soul to soul because almost all Native American poetry, whether it is a sacred chant or an individual's song, has a spiritual drift. A Yokuts poet in California longs to be "one with this world"; a Passamaquoddy poet in Maine celebrates "the song of the stars." There is always a sense of the sacred–so deeply rooted that some translators cannot see beyond it to the humor and humanity that are also so richly present.

The same qualities can be seen in the work of today's Native American poets, such as Joseph Bruchac, Linda Hogan, Ray A. Young Bear, Louise Erdrich, and Luci Tapahonso. Their writing moves us partly because of its deep roots in the Native American song traditions that this book explores.

Early translators tried to express these traditions in conventional verse forms. These attempts, while they have their own beauties, tend to ornament the directness of the original texts. Brevity is the essence of most Native American songs; the weight of meaning gains authority and power with each repetition of a line or phrase, with each rearrangement of beloved words.

The collector Natalie Curtis once asked a Native American poet which came first, words or music. "The Indian stared at me in puzzled surprise: 'I made a song,' he answered, 'a song is words and music–all comes together.'" It is our luck that people such as Natalie Curtis and Frances Densmore, understanding this, paid close attention to the music in and behind the words when translating such songs into English poems.

Frances Densmore–who devoted her life to recording and understanding Native American song–wrote that Indian poetry was marked by "rhythm, beauty, and mystery." All three of these qualities are abundantly represented in this anthology, and matched in the breathtaking photographs by Edward S. Curtis.

I have arranged the poems in a circle, from dawn to dawn, in recognition of the truth expressed by Hehaka Sapa, or Black Elk, of the Teton Sioux: "You have noticed that everything an Indian does is in a circle, and that is because the Power of the World always works in circles, and everything tries to be round."

Neil Philip

Crying to the Spirits *Hidatsa*

Earth Always Endures

Earth

       always

       endures.

Mandan

Sung by Wounded Face (Paii')

TRANSLATED BY FRANCES DENSMORE

Offering to the Sun *Tewa*

Magpie Song

The magpie! The magpie! Here underneath
In the white of his wings are the footsteps of morning.
        It dawns! It dawns!

Navajo

TRANSLATED BY WASHINGTON MATTHEWS

Prayer at Sunrise

Now this day
My sun father,
Now that you have come out standing to your sacred place,
That from which we draw the water of life,
Prayer meal,
Here I give to you.
Your long life,
Your old age,
Your waters,
Your seeds,
Your riches,
Your power
Your strong spirit,
All these to me may you grant.

Zuñi

TRANSLATED BY RUTH L. BUNZEL

Song of the Opening of the Shrine

He is about to come into the light of day,
Let him be touched with gentle hands.

He is about to come into the light of day,
He will turn himself from side to side.

He is about to come into the light of day,
Let the cord of the mouth be untied.

He is about to come into the light of day,
Let the mouth be opened wide.

He is about to come into the light of day,
Let him pass through and be born.

He is about to come into the light of day,
Let him be taken with gentle hands.

Osage

Sung by Saucy-calf (Tse-zhin'-ga-wa-da-in-ga)

TRANSLATED BY FRANCIS LA FLESCHE

A Flathead Mother *Flathead*

The Child Is Introduced to the Cosmos at Birth

Ho! Ye Sun, Moon, Stars, all ye that move in the heavens,
>   I bid you hear me!
Into your midst has come a new life.
>   Consent ye, I implore!
Make its path smooth, that it may reach the brow of the first hill!

Ho! Ye Winds, Clouds, Rain, Mist, all ye that move in the air,
>   I bid you hear me!
Into your midst has come a new life.
>   Consent ye, I implore!
Make its path smooth, that it may reach the brow of the second hill!

Ho! Ye Hills, Valleys, Rivers, Lakes, Trees, Grasses, all ye of the earth,
>   I bid you hear me!
Into your midst has come a new life.
>   Consent ye, I implore!
Make its path smooth, that it may reach the brow of the third hill!

Ho! Ye Birds, great and small, that fly in the air,
Ho! Ye Animals, great and small, that dwell in the forest,
Ho! Ye Insects that creep among the grasses and burrow in the ground—
>   I bid you hear me!
Into your midst has come a new life.
>   Consent ye, I implore!
Make its path smooth, that it may reach the brow of the fourth hill.

Ho! All ye of the heavens, all ye of the air, all ye of the earth:

      I bid you all to hear me!

Into your midst has come a new life.

      Consent ye, consent ye all, I implore!

Make its path smooth – then shall it travel beyond the four hills!

Omaha

TRANSLATED BY ALICE C. FLETCHER & FRANCIS LA FLESCHE

An Absároke Child *Crow*

Song of the Sky Loom

O our Mother the Earth, O our Father the Sky,
Your children are we, and with tired backs
We bring you the gifts that you love.
Then weave for us a garment of brightness:
May the warp be the white light of morning,
May the weft be the red light of evening,
May the fringes be the falling rain,
May the border be the standing rainbow.
Thus weave for us a garment of brightness,
That we may walk fittingly where birds sing,
That we may walk fittingly where grass is green,
O our Mother the Earth, O our Father the sky.

Tewa

TRANSLATED BY HERBERT JOSEPH SPINDEN

The Blanket Weaver *Navajo*

Prayer to the Mystery *Oglala Sioux*

Prayer to the Goddess

Stenátliha, you are good, I pray for a long life.

I pray for your good looks,

I pray for good breath,

I pray for good speech.

I pray for feet like yours to carry me through a long life,

I pray for a life like yours.

I walk with people, ahead of me all is well;

I pray for people to smile as long as I live.

I pray to live long.

I pray, I say, for a long life

      to live with you where the good people are.

I live in poverty.

I wish the people there to speak of goodness and to talk to me.

I wish you to divide your good things with me, as a brother.

Ahead of me is goodness. Lead me on.

Apache

TRANSLATED BY EDWARD S. CURTIS

Stenátliha (Woman without Parents)
is the chief goddess of the Apache.

from **Sayataca's Night Chant**

In order that my daylight fathers' rain-filled rooms,
May be filled with all kinds of clothing,
That their house may have a heart,
That even in his doorway
The shelled corn may be spilled before his door,
That beans may be spilled before his door,
That wheat may be spilled outside his door,
That the house may be full of little boys,
And little girls,
And men and women grown to maturity,
That in his house
Children may jostle one another in the doorway,
In order that it may be thus,
With two plume wands joined together,
I have consecrated the center of his roof.
Praying for whatever you wished,
Through the winter,
Through the summer,
Throughout the cycle of the months,
I have prayed for light for you.

Zuñi

TRANSLATED BY RUTH L. BUNZEL

A Zuñi Doorway *Zuñi*

The Wind Blows from the Sea

By the sandy water I breathe in the odor of the sea,
From there the wind comes and blows over the world.
By the sandy water I breathe in the odor of the sea,
From there the clouds come and rain falls over the world.

Papago
Sung by José Hendricks
TRANSLATED BY FRANCES DENSMORE

Invocation to the Rainmakers

Cover my earth mother four times with many flowers.
Let the heavens be covered with the banked-up clouds.
Let the earth be covered with fog; cover the earth with rains.
Great waters, rains, cover the earth. Lightning cover the earth.
Let thunder be heard over the earth; let thunder be heard;
Let thunder be heard over the six regions of the earth.

Zuñi
Sung by Nai'uchi
TRANSLATED BY MATILDA COXE STEVENSON

Oglala Girls *Oglala Sioux*

The Mockingbird's Song

Rain, people, rain!
The rain is all around us.
It is going to come pouring down,
And the summer will be fair to see,
The mockingbird has said so.

Tiwa

TRANSLATED BY JOHN COMFORT FILLMORE

Cañon de Chelly *Navajo*

28

Song of the Home God

The sacred blue corn seed I am planting,
In one night it will grow and flourish,
In one night the corn increases,
In the garden of the Home God.

The sacred white corn seed I am planting,
In one day it will grow and ripen,
In one day the corn increases,
In its beauty it increases.

Navajo
TRANSLATED BY WASHINGTON MATTHEWS

Qastceqogan, who speaks this verse, is the Navajo god of home and farm.
His dwelling is at Broad Rock in the Cañon de Chelly, Arizona.

My Words Are Tied in One

My words are tied in one
With the great mountains,
With the great rocks,
With the great trees,
In one with my body
And my heart.

Do you all help me
With supernatural power,
And you, day,
And you, night!
All of you see me
One with this world!

Yokuts

TRANSLATED BY A. L. KROEBER

These two stanzas are the conclusion of
a Yokuts prayer, which has earlier invoked
seven Yokuts gods.

Hollow Horn Bear *Brulé Sioux*

31

Cutting the Center Pole *Cheyenne*

Song to the Trees and Streams

Dark against the sky yonder distant line
Lies before us. Trees we see, long the line of trees,
Bending, swaying in the breeze.

Bright with flashing light yonder distant line
Runs before us, swiftly runs, swift the river runs,
Winding, flowing o'er the land.

Hark. Oh, hark. A sound, yonder distant sound
Comes to greet us, singing comes, soft the river's song,
Rippling gently 'neath the trees.

Pawnee

Sung by Tahirussawichi

TRANSLATED BY ALICE C. FLETCHER

My Music Reaches to the Sky

My music
>> reaches
>> to the sky.

Chippewa
Sung by Ga'tcitcigi'cig
TRANSLATED BY FRANCES DENSMORE

Friendly Song

The sky
>> loves to hear me.

Chippewa
Sung by Wabezic'
TRANSLATED BY FRANCES DENSMORE

An Overhanging Cloud

An overhanging
>> cloud
>> repeats my words with pleasing sound.

Chippewa
Sung by Ki'miwûn
TRANSLATED BY FRANCES DENSMORE

Storytelling *Apache*

Wind Song

Wind now commences to sing;
       Wind now commences to sing.
The land stretches before me,
       Before me stretches away.

Wind's house now is thundering;
       Wind's house now is thundering.
I go roaring over the land,
       The land covered with thunder.

Over the windy mountains;
       Over the windy mountains,
Came the myriad-legged wind;
       The wind came running hither.

The Black Snake Wind came to me;
       The Black Snake Wind came to me,
Came and wrapped itself about,
       Came here running with its song.

Pima

Sung by Ha-ata

TRANSLATED BY FRANK RUSSELL

The Storm *Apache*

Song of the Thunders

Sometimes
    I go about pitying
    myself
    while I am carried by the wind
    across the sky.

Chippewa
Sung by Ga'gandac'
TRANSLATED BY FRANCES DENSMORE

Song of the Trees

The wind
    only
    I am afraid of.

Chippewa
Sung by Ga'gandac'
TRANSLATED BY FRANCES DENSMORE

Need I Be Afraid?

I am simply on the earth.
    Need I be afraid?

Hidatsa
Sung by Good Bear (Nahpi'tsitsakis)
TRANSLATED BY FRANCES DENSMORE

A Chippewa Tipi Among the Aspens *Chippewa*

Drying Pottery *Hopi*

Rattlesnake Ceremony Song

The king snake said to the rattlesnake:

Do not touch me!

You can do nothing with me.

Lying with your belly full,

Rattlesnake of the rock pile,

Do not touch me!

There is nothing you can do,

You rattlesnake with your belly full,

Lying where the ground squirrel holes are thick.

Do not touch me!

What can you do to me?

Rattlesnake in the tree clump,

Stretched in the shade,

You can do nothing;

Do not touch me!

Rattlesnake of the plains,

You whose white eye

The sun shines on,

Do not touch me!

Yokuts

TRANSLATED BY A. L. KROEBER

Ghost Dance Songs

I

Our father, the Whirlwind,
Our father, the Whirlwind,
Now wears the headdress of crow feathers,
Now wears the headdress of crow feathers.

II

My children, my children,
The wind makes the head-feathers sing–
The wind makes the head-feathers sing–
My children, my children.

III

Father have pity on me,
Father have pity on me,
I am crying for thirst,
I am crying for thirst;
All is gone–I have nothing to eat,
All is gone–I have nothing to eat.

IV

Father, the Morning Star!
Father, the Morning Star!
Look on us, we have danced until daylight,
Look on us, we have danced until daylight.
Take pity on us–*Hi-i-i!*
Take pity on us–*Hi-i-i!*

Arapaho

TRANSLATED BY JAMES MOONEY

Dancing to Restore an Eclipsed Moon *Qáqyuhl*

Because I Am Poor

Because I am poor,
I pray for every living creature.

Kiowa
TRANSLATED BY JAMES MOONEY

Let Me See, Is This Real?

Let me see, is this real,
Let me see, is this real,
Let me see, is this real,
This life I am living?
You who possess the skies,
Let me see, is this real,
This life I am living?

Pawnee
Song of the Iruska Society
TRANSLATED BY JAMES R. MURIE & DANIEL G. BRINTON

Woísta, Cheyenne Woman *Cheyenne*

Wishram Bride *Chinook*

46

When You Return

You may
　　　　go on the warpath.
When
　　　　you return
　　　　I will marry you.

Teton Sioux

Sung by Siya'ka

TRANSLATED BY FRANCES DENSMORE

Arikara Medicine Ceremony–The Buffalo *Arikara*

Song of the Rising of the Buffalo Bull Men

I rise, I rise,
I, whose tread makes the earth to rumble.

I rise, I rise,
I, in whose thighs there is strength.

I rise, I rise,
I, who whips his back with his tail when in rage.

I rise, I rise,
I, in whose humped shoulder there is power.

I rise, I rise,
I, who shakes his mane when angered.

I rise, I rise,
I, whose horns are sharp and curved.

Osage

Sung by Wa-xthi'-zhi

TRANSLATED BY FRANCIS LA FLESCHE

To the Buffalo

Strike ye now our land with your great curvèd horns;
In your mighty rage toss the turf in the air.
Strike ye now our land with your great curvèd horns;
We will hear the sound and our hearts will be strong.
When we go to war,
Give us of your strength in the time of our need,
King of all the plain–buffalo, buffalo.
Strike ye now our land with your great curvèd horns;
Lead us forth to fight.

Chippewa

TRANSLATED BY FRANCES DENSMORE

As It Was in the Old Days *Plains*

51

Oglala War Party *Oglala Sioux*

War Songs

I

Hear my voice, Birds of War!
I prepare a feast for you to feed on;
I see you cross the enemy's lines;
Like you I shall go.
I wish the swiftness of your wings;
I wish the vengeance of your claws;
I muster my friends;
I follow your flight.
Ho, you young men warriors,
Bear your angers in the place of fighting!

II

From the south they came, Birds of War–
Hark! to their passing scream.
I wish the body of the fiercest,
As swift, as cruel, as strong.
I cast my body to the chance of fighting.
Happy I shall be to lie in that place,
In that place where the fight was,
Beyond the enemy's line.

III

Here on my breast have I bled!
See–see! My battle scars!
Ye mountains, tremble at my yell!
I strike for life.

Chippewa

TRANSLATED BY HENRY ROWE SCHOOLCRAFT

A Spell to Destroy Life

Listen! Now I have come to step over your soul.
       You are of the [Wolf] clan.
       Your name is [A'yu'nini].
Your spittle I have put at rest under the earth.
Your soul I have put at rest under the earth.
I have come to cover you over with the black rock.
I have come to cover you over with the black cloth.
I have come to cover you over with the black slabs,
       never to reappear.
Toward the black coffin of the upland in the Darkening Land
       your path shall stretch out.
So shall it be for you.

The clay of the upland has come to cover you.
Instantly the black clay has lodged there where it is at rest
       at the black houses in the Darkening Land.
With the black coffin and with the black slabs I have come to cover you.
       Now your soul has faded away.
       It has become blue.
When darkness comes your spirit shall grow less, and dwindle away,
       never to reappear.
Listen!

Cherokee

Sung by A'yu'nini (Swimmer)

TRANSLATED BY JAMES MOONEY

The clan name and personal name would change,
depending on the target of this much-feared spell.

Piegan Riders *Piegan*

Love Song

All my heart is lonely,
All my heart is full of sorrow.
My lover, my lover is departed.

Dark the sky at evening,
Sad the bird notes in the dawning.
My lover, my lover is departed.

He was all my sunshine,
His the beauty and the gladness.
Return, return, gladness and joy.

Chippewa

TRANSLATED BY FRANCES DENSMORE

Cree Girl *Cree*

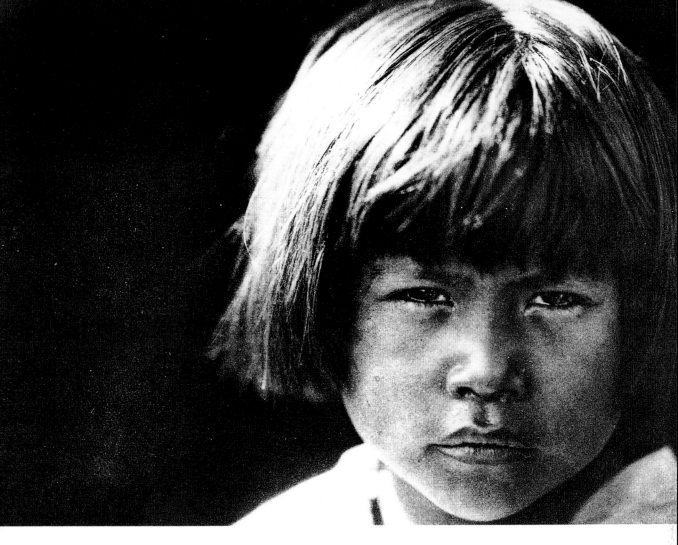

Comanche Girl *Comanche*

Wind Song

I have but one love,
I have but one love,
I have but one love,
And he is far away,
On the warpath, *e-ye, e-eye!*
Lonely are the days, and weary.

Kiowa

Sung by Eagle Chief (T'e-ne-t'e)

TRANSLATED BY NATALIE CURTIS

Song of an Ambitious Mother

This I have come to ask you,
This I have come to ask you–
      O, let your daughter
      Marry my son, the hunter,
      And he'll give your daughter
      My big brass kettle.

Chippewa

Sung by Double Sky Woman (Bi'tawagi'jigo'kwe)

TRANSLATED BY FRANCES DENSMORE

Warpath Song

Ah, I never, never can forget
The playful word you spoke long since.
This man who seeks to marry me,
He with his sore-backed ponies,
      What's he to me?

Kiowa

Sung by Eagle Chief (T'e-ne-t'e)

TRANSLATED BY NATALIE CURTIS

Nespelim Girl *Sanpoil*

Song of Entering the Village

I am home, I am home, I am home,
I have now come to the land that is home.
I have now come to the border of the village.
I have now come to the foot-worn soil of the village.
I have now come to the rear of the sacred house.
I have now come to the end of the sacred house.
I have now come to the door of the sacred house.
I have now come inside of the sacred house.
I have now come to the kettle pole of the sacred house.
I have now come to the fireplace of the sacred house.
I have now come to the middle of the sacred house.
I have now come to the smoke vent of the sacred house.
I have now come into the midst of the light of day.

Osage
Sung by Wa-xthi'-zhi

TRANSLATED BY FRANCIS LA FLESCHE

Blackfoot Tipis *Blackfoot*

On Presenting an Enemy-slayer with a Cup of Water

Within my bowl there lies
Shining dizziness,
Bubbling drunkenness.

There are great whirlwinds
Standing upside down above us.
They lie within my bowl.

A great bear heart,
A great eagle heart,
A great hawk heart,
A great twisting wind–
All these have gathered here
And lie within my bowl.

Now you will drink it.

Papago

TRANSLATED BY RUTH MURRAY UNDERHILL

A warrior who had slain an enemy remained in seclusion
for many days afterward, until he was purified.
He drank from a new cup, which was thrown away every four days.

Two Moons *Cheyenne*

I Will Walk

I will walk into somebody's dwelling,
Into somebody's dwelling will I walk.
To thy dwelling, my dearly beloved,
Some night will I walk, will I walk.
Some night in the winter, my beloved
To thy dwelling will I walk, will I walk.
This very night, my beloved,
To thy dwelling will I walk, will I walk.

Chippewa

TRANSLATED BY HENRY ROWE SCHOOLCRAFT

Camp in the Cottonwoods *Cheyenne*

Buffalo Berry Gatherers *Mandan*

Mashing the Berries

I am mashing the berries,
I am mashing the berries.
They say travelers are coming on the march.

I stir the berries around,
I stir them around.
I take them up with a spoon of buffalo horn.

And I carry them,
I carry them to the strangers.
And I carry them,
I carry them to the strangers.

Kiowa

TRANSLATED BY JAMES MOONEY

The Noise of the Village

Whenever I pause
      the noise
      of the village.

Chippewa
Sung by Ki'miwûn
TRANSLATED BY FRANCES DENSMORE

When I Was Young

When I was young, I took no heed;
      Old, old, I have become!
Because I knew that age would come
      To me, I took no heed.

Chiricahua Apache
TRANSLATED BY MORRIS EDWARD OPLER

Professor Opler's informant told him, "Many
years ago I saw an old man sitting by the fire
working. He sang this song then, and, as he
sang it, the tears rolled down his cheeks. He
was thinking back to the good times he had
when he was a young man. It's really an old
man's song. They just sit there in a pitiful way
and sing it slowly. I can't sing it like that."

The Entire World

The entire
      world
      weeps for me.

Chippewa
Sung by Ki'miwûn
TRANSLATED BY FRANCES DENSMORE

Chief Joseph *Nez Percé*

Winter *Crow*

I Heard You

Finally you have cried. I heard you.
Finally you have cried. I heard you.
Finally you have cried. I heard you.
Finally you have cried. I heard you.

This earth you have made me hear.
Finally you have cried.
You have made me hear.
You have made me hear.

This day you have made me hear.
Finally you have cried.
You have made me hear.
You have made me hear.

Winnebago

Song of the Buffalo Clan

TRANSLATED BY PAUL RADIN

Wolf *Crow*

72

A Wolf I Considered Myself

A wolf

        I considered myself

        but

        I have eaten nothing,

        therefore

        from standing

        I am tired out.

A wolf

        I considered myself

        but

        the owls are hooting

        and

        the night I fear.

Teton Sioux

Sung by Gray Hawk (Cetan'-hota)

TRANSLATED BY FRANCES DENSMORE

I Am a Wolf

I am a lonely wolf, wandering pretty much nearly all over the world

     He, he, he!

What is the matter? I am having a hard time, friend.

This that I tell you, you will have to do also.

Whatever I want, I always get it.

Your name will be big, as mine is big. *Hiu! Hiu!*

Teton Sioux

Sung by Sitting Bull

TRANSLATED BY W. S. CAMPBELL

Sitting Bull was taught this song by a wolf, whose howl – *Hiu!* – ends the song.

Song of Sitting Bull

A warrior
      I have been;
      now
      it is all over.
A hard time
      I have.

Teton Sioux

Sung by Used-as-a-Shield (Waha'canka-ya'pi)

TRANSLATED BY FRANCES DENSMORE

The Death Song of White Antelope

Nothing lives long
Nothing lives long
Nothing lives long
Only the earth and the mountains.

Cheyenne

Sung by White Antelope

TRANSLATED BY GEORGE BENT

White Antelope, a noted Cheyenne war leader,
was murdered at the infamous Sand Creek
Massacre of 1864, as he stood, arms folded,
singing this song. Over a hundred and
fifty Cheyenne were slaughtered at dawn by
the Colorado volunteers, and their bodies
mutilated.

Slow Bull *Oglala Sioux*

Sun Dance Pledgers *Cheyenne*

76

I Am Walking

Toward calm and shady places
        I am walking
      on the earth.

Chippewa
Sung by Maiñ'ans
TRANSLATED BY FRANCES DENSMORE

Song of Two Ghosts

My friend
        this is a wide world
        we're traveling over
        walking on the moonlight.

Omaha
Sung by Little Dancer
TRANSLATED BY REO FRANKLIN FORTUNE

The Song of the Stars

We are the stars which sing,
We sing with our light.
We are the birds of fire
We fly over the sky,
Our light is a voice.
We make a road for spirits,
For the spirits to pass over.
Among us are three hunters
Who chase a bear;
There never was a time
When they were not hunting.
We look down on the mountains.
This is the song of the stars.

Passamaquoddy

TRANSLATED BY CHARLES GODFREY LELAND

Apache Land *Apache*

The Heavens Are Speaking

I stood here, I stood there,
The clouds are speaking,
I say, "You are the ruling power,
I do not understand, I only know what I am told,
You are the ruling power, you who are now speaking,
This power is yours, O heavens."

Pawnee

Sung by John Luwak (Laduda Desadu, He-Does-Everything-as-a-Chief)

TRANSLATED BY FRANCES DENSMORE

Our Hearts Are Set in the Heavens

It is there that our hearts are set,
In the expanse of the heavens.

Pawnee

Sung by Effie Blain (Tsastawinahiigat, She-Led-a-Pony-into-the-Ceremony)

TRANSLATED BY FRANCES DENSMORE

These two songs belonged to Man Chief, chief
of the four bands of the Pawnee, who died in 1858.

80

Mósa *Mohave*

81

A Blackfoot Woman *Blackfoot*

In the Blue Night

How shall I begin my song
In the blue night that is settling?
I will sit here and begin my song.

Brown Owls

Brown owls come here in the blue evening,
They are hooting about,
They are shaking their wings and hooting.

In the Great Night

In the great night my heart will go out,
Toward me the darkness comes rattling,
In the great night my heart will go out.

Papago

Sung by Sivariano Garcia

TRANSLATED BY FRANCES DENSMORE

These three songs belonged to Owl Woman,
a healer, known as Juana Maxwell, who
received the last in a dream from the spirit
of José Gomez.

A Lullaby

Go to sleep,
Go to sleep,
Lest something come,
To take away
My little one.
So you must sleep,
My little one.

Tewa
TRANSLATED BY HERBERT JOSEPH SPINDEN

Last Daylight Song

Lullaby, lullaby.
It is daybreak. Lullaby.
Now comes the Daylight Boy. Lullaby.
Now it is day. Lullaby.
Now comes the Daylight Girl. Lullaby.

Navajo
TRANSLATED BY WASHINGTON MATTHEWS

Achomawi Mother and Child *Achomawi*

Songs of Life Returning

I

The wind stirs the willows.
The wind stirs the grasses.

II

The cottonwoods are growing tall,
They are growing tall and verdant.

III

Fog! Fog!
Lightning! Lightning!
Whirlwind! Whirlwind!

IV

The whirlwind! The whirlwind!
The snowy earth comes gliding,
The snowy earth comes gliding.

V

There is dust from the whirlwind,
There is dust from the whirlwind,
The whirlwind on the mountain.

VI

The rocks are ringing,
The rocks are ringing,
They are ringing in the mountains.

Paiute

Ghost Dance songs

TRANSLATED BY JAMES MOONEY

Kindling Fire *Assiniboin*

All Is Restored in Beauty

The world before me is restored in beauty,
The world behind me is restored in beauty,
The world below me is restored in beauty,
The world above me is restored in beauty,
My voice is restored in beauty.
It is restored in beauty.
It is restored in beauty.
It is restored in beauty.
It is restored in beauty.

Navajo

TRANSLATED BY WASHINGTON MATTHEWS

Riders in the Twilight *Navajo*

I Am Like a Bear

I am like a bear,
      I hold up my hands
      waiting for the sun to rise.

Pawnee
Sung by Dog Chief
TRANSLATED BY FRANCES DENSMORE

Arikara Medicine Ceremony–The Bears *Arikara*

Song at Sunrise

Here am I
        behold me,
        I am the sun
        behold me.

Teton Sioux
Sung by Red Bird (Zintka'la-lu'ta)
TRANSLATED BY FRANCES DENSMORE

Snake Song

Fire
        inside me
Soul
        inside me.

Chippewa
Sung by George Farmer (Ne-ba-day-ke-shi-go-kay)
TRANSLATED BY ALBERT B. REAGAN

Sources

PHOTOGRAPHS

All the photographs in this book are taken from the 20 volumes and accompanying plate portfolios of *The North American Indian* by Edward S. Curtis, published in a limited edition, 1907–30, and reproduced by permission of The British Library (shelfmarks +° L. R. 298. a. 23, L. R. 298. b. 2).

POEMS

Copyright © material is reprinted by permission of the publishers. Material from the Bureau of American Ethnology (B.A.E.) reprinted by kind permission of the Smithsonian Institution Press, Washington, D.C.

Brinton, Daniel G. *Essays of an Americanist*. Philadelphia: Porter & Coates, 1890. "Let Me See, Is This Real?" **Bunzel**, Ruth L. *Zuñi Ritual Poetry*. Washington: Smithsonian Institution Press, B.A.E. 47th Annual Report, © 1932. "Prayer at Sunrise," *"from Sayataca's Night Chant."* **Campbell**, W. S. ("Stanley Vestal"). *Sitting Bull, Champion of the Sioux*. Boston & New York: Houghton Mifflin Company, © 1932. "I Am a Wolf." **Curtis**, Edward S. *The American Indian*, vol. 1. Cambridge, Mass.: The University Press, 1907. "Prayer to the Goddess." **Curtis**, Natalie. *The Indians' Book*. New York & London: Harper & Brothers, 1907, 1923. "Wind Song" (Kiowa), "War-path Song." **Densmore**, Frances. *Chippewa Music*. Washington: B.A.E. Bulletin 45, 1910. "I Am Walking," "Song of the Trees," "Song of the Thunders," "My Music Reaches to the Sky," "Friendly Song." *Chippewa Music II*. Washington: B.A.E. Bulletin 53, 1913. "An Overhanging Cloud," "The Noise of the Village," "The Entire World." *Mandan and Hidatsa Music*. Washington: B.A.E. Bulletin 80, © 1923. "Earth Always Endures," "Need I Be Afraid?" *Papago Music*. Washington: B.A.E. Bulletin 90, © 1929. "Brown Owls," "In the Blue Night," "In the Great Night," "The Wind Blows from the Sea." *Pawnee Music*. Washington: B.A.E. Bulletin 93, © 1929. "I Am Like a Bear," "Our Hearts Are Set in the Heavens," "The Heavens Are Speaking." *Poems from Sioux and Chippewa Songs*. Washington: Privately Printed, 1917. "To the Buffalo," "Love Song," "Song of an Ambitious Mother." *Teton Sioux Music*. Washington: B.A.E. Bulletin 61, 1918. "When You Return," "A Wolf I Considered Myself," "Song of Sitting Bull," "Song at Sunrise." **Fletcher**, Alice Cunningham. *The Hako: A Pawnee Ceremony*. Washington: B.A.E. 22nd Annual Report, 1904. "Song to the Trees and Streams." *Indian Song and Story from North America*. Boston: Small Maynard, 1900. "The Mocking-bird's Song." **Fletcher**, Alice Cunningham, and **La Flesche**, Francis. *The Omaha Tribe*. Washington: B.A.E. 27th Annual Report, 1911. "The Child Is Introduced to the Cosmos at Birth." **Fortune**, Reo Franklin. *Omaha Secret Societies*. New York: Columbia University Press, © 1932. "Song of Two Ghosts." **Hyde**, George E. *Life of George Bent: Written from His Letters*. Norman: University of Oklahoma Press, 1968. "The Death Song of White Antelope." **Kroeber**, A. L. *Handbook of the Indians of California*. Washington: B.A.E. Bulletin 78, © 1925. "My Words Are Tied in One," "Rattlesnake Ceremony Song." **La Flesche**, Francis. *The Osage Tribe: The Rite of Vigil*. Washington: B.A.E. 39th Annual Report, © 1925. "Song of the Opening of the Shrine." *The Osage Tribe: Songs of the Wa-xó-be*. Washington: B.A.E. 45th Annual Report, © 1930. "Song of the Rising of the Buffalo Bull Men." *War Ceremony and Peace Ceremony of the Osage Indians*. Washington: B.A.E. Bulletin 101, © 1939. "Song of Entering the Village." **Leland**, Charles Godfrey. *The Algonquin Legends of New England*. Boston: Houghton, Mifflin and Company, 1884. "The Song of the Stars." **Matthews**, Washington. *The Mountain Chant, A Navaho Ceremony*. Washington: B.A.E. 5th Annual Report, 1887. "Last Daylight Song." *Navaho Gambling Songs*, in *American Anthropologist* vol. 2 (O.S.). Washington: Anthropological Society of Wisconsin, 1889. "Magpie Song." *Songs of Sequence of the Navahos*, in *Journal of American Folklore* vol. 7. Boston: American Folklore Society, 1894. "Song of the Home God." *The Prayer of a Navaho Shaman*, in American Anthropologist vol. 2 (O.S.), 1889. "All Is Restored in Beauty." **Mooney**, James. *The Ghost-Dance Religion*. Washington: B.A.E. 14th Annual Report, 1896. "Ghost Dance Songs," "Because I Am Poor," "Mashing the Berries," "Songs of Life Returning." *The Sacred Formulas of the Cherokees*. Washington: B.A.E. 7th Annual Report, 1891. "A Spell to Destroy Life." **Opler**, Morris Edward. *An Apache Life-Way*. Chicago: The University of Chicago Press, © 1941. "When I Was Young." **Radin**, Paul. *The Winnebago Tribe*. Washington: B.A.E. 37th Annual Report, © 1923. "I Heard You." **Reagan**, A. B. *Medicine Songs of George Farmer*, in *American Anthropologist* vol. 24 (N.S.). Menasha, Wisconsin: American Anthropological Association, 1922. "Snake Song." **Russell**, Frank. *The Pima Indians*. Washington: B.A.E. 26th Annual Report, 1908. "Wind Song" (Pima). **Schoolcraft**, Henry Rowe. *Historical and Statistical Information Respecting the Indian Tribes of the United States*. Philadelphia: Lippincott, Grambo, 1851-57. "War Songs," "I Will Walk." **Spinden**, Herbert Joseph. *Songs of the Tewa*. New York: The Exposition of Tribal Arts, Inc., 1933. "A Lullaby," "Song of the Sky Loom." **Stevenson**, Matilda Coxe. *The Zuñi Indians*. Washington: B.A.E. 23rd Annual Report, 1904. "Invocation to the Rain-makers." **Underhill**, Ruth Murray. *Singing for Power: The Song Magic of the Papago Indians of Southern Arizona*. Berkeley: University of California Press, © 1938, 1966. "On Presenting an Enemy-slayer with a Cup of Water."

Further Reading

THE NATIVE AMERICANS

Griffin-Pierce, Trudy. *The Encyclopedia of Native America.* New York: Viking, 1995.
Hausman, Gerald. *Turtle Island Alphabet: A Lexicon of Native American Symbols and Culture.* New York: St. Martin's Press, 1993.
Josephy, Alvin M. *500 Nations: An Illustrated History of North American Indians.* New York: Alfred A. Knopf, 1994.
Swanton, John R. *The Indian Tribes of North America.* Washington: B.A.E. Bulletin 145, 1952.

NATIVE AMERICAN POETRY

Brandon, William. *The Magic World.* New York: William Morrow & Company, 1971.
Cronyn, George. *The Path on the Rainbow.* New York: Liveright Publishing Corporation, 1918, 1934. Reissued as *American Indian Poetry.* New York: Fawcett Columbine, 1991.
Day, A. Grove. *The Sky Clears.* Lincoln: University of Nebraska Press, 1951.
Howard, Helen Addison. *American Indian Poetry.* New York: Twayne, 1979.
Niatum, Duane. *Harper's Anthology of 20th Century Native American Poetry.* San Francisco: HarperCollins, 1988.
Rothenberg, Jerome. *Shaking the Pumpkin.* Garden City, N.Y.: Doubleday, 1972.

EDWARD SHERIFF CURTIS

Curtis, Edward S. *Portraits from the North American Indian.* New York: Dutton, 1972. *Native Nations.* Boston: Bulfinch Press, 1993. *Prayer to the Great Mystery.* New York: St. Martin's Press, 1995.
Davis, Barbara. *Edward S. Curtis: The Life and Times of a Shadow Catcher.* San Francisco: Chronicle Books, 1985.

Wishram Basket Worker *Chinook*